31
SUPERNATURAL FELINES

31 Supernatural Felines (Illustrated Foklore, Book 4)

Copyright © 2024 by Alex Kujawa

All rights reserved. No part of this book may be reproduced or utilized in any form or by any means, electronic or mechanical, including photocopying, recording, or by any information storage and retrieval system, without permission in writing from the authors, except in the case of brief excerpts or quotations embodied in critical articles and reviews.

Art & Graphic Design by Alex Kujawa
Written by Alex Kujawa & Scott Wheeler
Edited by Scott Wheeler

First Printing: April 2022
Second Edition June 2024
ISBN 979-8-9866079-4-8

Wheejawa Publishing
PO Box 601
WOOD DALE, IL 60191-2094
www.AlexKujawa.com

For my beloved first cat Quistis,
and for all the cat lovers out there.

31 Supernatural Felines
an illustrated folklore book

ALEX KUJAWA
WITH SCOTT WHEELER

Wheejawa
Publishing
2024

From the Artist:

This is the fourth book in what I now refer to as my folklore series, something that began as an art project for an annual October art event known as Inktober, during which artists from all over the world challenge themselves to post one new piece of art per day on social media. I started participating in this art event as early as 2014, but in 2017 I decided I was ready for a more intense project. At that time, I was interested in finding more about female folklore creatures from around the world, and thus my first book "31 Female Ghosts, Monsters, and Demons from Around the World" was born after a friend convinced me to publish the art project for others to enjoy. I myself enjoyed the research, art, and book design so much I have been making more of these since then.

31 SUPERNATURAL FELINES is a collection of drawings, the majority of which were completed in October of 2021. My goal of the research for this book was finding as many interesting folklore cat creatures from around the world as I could, and then choosing 31 to draw and tell you all about. Though I have to admit that I have a particular interest in Slavic folklore, based on my own origin, and thus you'll find quite a lot of Slavic cats in here.

Much research and love was put in to creating this little book. Thank you for purchasing it, I hope you will enjoy it.

GUMIENNIK Slavic	1
KOSZKI Slavic	2
CHA KLA Thai	3
GNIECIUCH Slavic	4
CAT-SITH Celtic	5
BAKENEKO Japanese	6
NEKOMATA Chinese/Japanese	7
MRUCEK Slavic	8
LYNX Greek	9
MIAWKI Slavic	10
MATAGOT French/Spanish	11
BALL-TAILED CAT North American	12
PANTHER Greek/European	13
POPIELNIK Slavic	14
CHOCHLIK Slavic	15
BASTET Egyptian	16
WAG-BY-THE-WAY Celtic	17
CATH PALUG Celtic	18
YULE CAT Icelandic	19
WARGIN Slavic	20
KASHA Japanese	21
CACTUS CAT North American	22
MANEKI-NEKO Japanese	23
UNDERWATER PANTHER Native North American	24
BAYUN Slavic	25
DEMON CAT North American	26
MAJKI Slavic	27
SPLINTERCAT North American	28
PAUCA BILLEE Indian/World	29
WAMPUS Native North American	30
BOG CAT Celtic	31

GUMIENNIK
Origin: Slavic

Their name comes from the old Polish "gumno" which was a name given to the main yard and all the outbuildings of a farm, including the barn where the grain was stored. Gumiennik was a type of a Slavic guardian spirit that took care of the grain and protected the estate. It lived in a barn and usually took the form of a black barn cat. It would protect the grain from fires (by putting them out), thieves (by chasing them away), and pests (by hunting and killing them). If angered, however, Gumiennik could turn on the estate and destroy the grain, sometimes even burning down the whole barn. Apparently in the olden days, old Slavic folk would cut off the tip of a cat's tail to remove venom they believed resided there, however if this was done to Gumiennik, a disaster was ensured.

Other Names:
Ovinnik, Jownik, Joŭnik

KOSZKI
Origin: Slavic

Creatures of Slavic folklore, Koszki were often mistaken for regular cats – small in stature, they had very thick fur, long sticking up ears, a thick tail, walked on all fours, and mewed like cats when speaking. However, if you look into their faces through the (usually black) fur, they had a grey humanoid visage underneath, and their front paws were in fact long boney hands. It was a disaster to let one of these in to your house, and it was best to closely examine any cats you intended to let inside. Koszki would find homes with new born babies and switch them with their own skinny, ugly offspring. Once a Koszki found a house it liked, it would try to break in to it. The only way to keep it out of it was to beat it up with a club made from oak wood.

Cha Kla
Origin: Thai

Cha Kla, meaning cat with dull black fur, is a cat ghost in Thai folklore, utilized by sorcerors as a weapon against their enemies. It can appear either as a house cat or a wild cat with eyes the color of blood, and its matte black fur runs from back-to-front. When not used by sorcerors, it is said to be nocturnal, and to hide in a hole in the ground during the daytime. They are generally fearful of humans, and will try to run and hide. A person who touches a Cha Kla or even sees it is said to be cursed with death.

Other Names:
Cha kla, Phi Cha kla

GNIECIUCH
Origin: Slavic

A Slavic folklore monster described as a small, furry, cat-like creature with very skinny long limbs, claws, and a big heavy stomach; but is usually invisible, choosing to appear mostly to intoxicated people. Sometimes it wears a red or golden cap in which it hides valuable coins. It likes to reside in cupboards of people's homes and comes out only at night. Gnieciuch are attracted to the smell of alcohol and enjoy sitting on the chests of sleeping people, smelling the alcohol off their breath, sometimes going far enough to actually suck blood off those people to become intoxicated themselves. Those who had a Gnieciuch visit them in their sleep will wake up completely exhausted with aches all over their bodies from the heavy weight of the creature sitting on them the whole night. To protect yourself from Gnieciuch, one must obtain a special chalk that has been blessed (świecona kreda), and draw a circle around your bed. This simple remedy may end up being quite difficult after a few shots of vodka though, and the Gnieciuch will still get you. It is effectively the Slavic cat-demon of hangovers.

OTHER NAMES:
Gniutek, Hurbóz, Gniot, Gniotek, Gnietek, Gnocek, Gnotek, Wiek

Cat-Sith

Origin: Celtic

A fae from Celtic mythology said to haunt the Highlands area of Scotland, the Cat-Sith (plural: Cait-Sith) usually takes the form of a black cat with a white spot on its chest. Sometimes said to be a witch that can transform in to a cat nine times, and would remain in cat form permanently after the ninth transformation. Local superstition held that Cait-Sith could steal the soul of a recently dead person by passing over that person's corpse. To prevent this, a watch was set on a fresh corpse night and day until burial could commence, in order to deter the Cait-Sith. The watch would engage in various activities to distract the Cait-Sith, including telling riddles, singing and playing musical instruments, wrestling, and laying catnip around the area. Fires would be avoided, as these were said to attract Cait-Sith.

Other Names:
Cat-sìth, cat sí, Sith Cat

BAKENEKO
Origin: Japanese

Bakeneko "monster cat" or "changed cat" is a cat yokai from Japan. It is said that as a cat grows old beyond a certain age, grows heavy beyond a certain weight, or has an especially long tail, that it will become a Bakeneko. This superstition has historically led to cats being not kept beyond a certain age or weight, or of cats tails being bobbed by their owners to prevent this transformation. Bakeneko can grow as large as a human or even larger, can shapeshift either in to human form or that of a smaller cat, and have been said to take the place of humans by impersonating them long-term. They will sometimes wrap their heads in towels or napkins as a disguise, to dance around, and to speak or sing as a human would. The Bakeneko seems to be almost a Japanese catch-all for mythical cat stories of Chinese origin, or perhaps the most recent common ancestor of all Japanese cat mythology and folklore, leading back to the original importation of cats to Japan by Buddhist monks seeking to protect their scrolls from damaging pests such as mice.

Origin: Chinese / Japanese

Nekomata or a "forked-tail cat", is a cat spirit of Chinese origin, viewed as a yokai in Japanese tradition, related to the Bakeneko. The Nekomata's distinguishing characteristic is its forked tail, double-tail, or just having two tails, which can occur not from birth but from an early age, where a young cat's tail splits, causing it to become a Nekomata. This may also happen to a Bakeneko that grows large enough and old enough, gaining more power in doing so. Nekomata have some overlap of characteristics and abilities with the Bakeneko, but more commonly are said to start fires with their tails and to reanimate corpses to use as puppets. They grow even larger than a Bakeneko, and are sometimes viewed as a more powerful, intelligent, and malicious version of the Bakeneko.

Mrucek
Origin: Slavic

A small house spirit that favors the warmest corners of the house, usually near a fireplace. Harmless, but also not very helpful, Mrucek spends most of it's time sleeping. If seen, it will look like a cat, but often it prefers to be invisible. You may hear a purring noise coming from somewhere in your house, but be unable to find the Mrucek making the noise. Another form Mrucek likes to take on, mainly for the purposes of scaring children away from bothering it, is that of a large humanoid head, resting on four legs, with wide lips and big ears.

Other Names:
Mruczek

Origin: Greek Mythology

The Lynx is a genus of wildcat found in Europe, Asia, and North America, whose various species have featured in the mythologies of the people from these lands. Its glowing (reflective) cat-eyes led it to be associated with supernatural eyesight. The phrase "Lynx-eyed" is equivalent to "Eagle-eyed" in modern English, and is notably present in modern-day Spanish (con ojos de lince). At least two characters in Greek mythology were known as Lynceus ("Lynx-eyed"), as well as the tale of King Lyncus (Lynkos) who was transformed in to a Lynx as punishment for plotting against the goddess Demeter. Theophrastus wrote that Lynx urine would harden in to a gemstone which was called lyngurium or ligurion (which was possibly related etymologically to amber and/or the Italian region of Liguria); and this belief regarding the stone was accepted as scientific for over a millenium thereafter. There is also a constellation of Lynx, described by Polish astronomer Johannes Hevelius, who challenged that the stars of the constellation were so faint that only those with Lynx-eyes would be able to see it clearly.

MIAWKI
Origin: Slavic

Miawki are small creatures from Slavic folklore that live in forests and are often seen during Springtime. From afar they are easily mistaken for human children, running around in flowering meadows and having an overall good time. Miawki have cat-like faces and blonde hair. They celebrate Springtime while mewing "May! May!" and happily dancing around in circles. They invite humans to join them, but it is usually a bad idea to accept. If you go in to the woods with Miawki, you will likely end up meeting other forest demons that are going to kill you.

OTHER NAMES:
Niawki

Matagot
Origin: French / Spanish

The Matagot (likely Spanish etymology meaning "killer of Christians") is an animal spirit originating from Southern France and parts of Spain. They can take the form of many animals, including that of a black cat, and are usually considered malevolent but can be beneficial under the correct circumstances. A matagot can be lured with an offering of meat, such as fresh chicken; the Matagot must then be carried to one's home without once looking behind you, and then kept well-fed indefinitely, usually by offering the matagot the first bites of everything you eat and the first sips of everything you drink. If this routine is successfully mantained, the owner of the Matagot will find a gold coin each morning. One must however be cautious to release the Matagot long before one's death, or the process of dying will be lengthy and tormentous owing to the evil nature of the Matagot.

Other Names:
Mantagot

Ball-Tailed Cat

Origin: North American

The Ball-Tailed Cat is a creature of North American folklore of "fearsome critter" tradition. These were essentially made-up tales of ridiculous creatures told as campfire stories, especially among loggers in the late 19th and early 20th centuries, some tales of which survive in certain regions to this day. The Ball-Tailed Cat was said to resemble a wildcat in overall size and shape, but that it had a weaponized heavy ball at the end of its tail, which was used to attack prey, including humans. Sometimes the ball was smooth, sometimes spiked, and sometimes one side of each. Tales of other cats with a similar or identical feature include the Silvercat and Dingmaul, and these are often associated with each other or seen as variants of the same creature. The Ball-Tailed Cat will perch in a tree, preparing to descend on to a human passing below, whom it would proceed to beat to death with its ball-tail. This behavior is similar to that of the "Drop-bear" which is a fictitious carnivorous koala tale told by unscrupulous Australian locals attempting to prank visiting tourists. A more direct connection between these transcontinental stories has not been established.

Other Names:
Felis caudaglobosa

 PANTHER
Origin: Ancient Greek / Medieval European

In several European mythologies, the Panther is a spotted mythical cat with a few peculiar characteristics. Described as having white or black spots like eyes, a multicolored coat, and a sweet and enticing smell. It goes in to a cycle of resting for three days after eating, after which it lets out a loud roar. The roar draws the attention of various creatures who then notice the pleasant smell, which they follow until they reach the panther, providing it with its next meal. Only the dragon has the ability to stay away from the pleasant smell, and the Panther's roar is a sign to the dragon to run away and hide. Of all animals, apparently only the dragon is enemy to the mythical Panther. The Panther emblem in heraldly is derived from these medieval and classical myths.

Other Names:
Pantera, Pantere, Love Cervere

POPIELNIK
Origin: Slavic

During Slavic pagan times, Popielnik was an ancient immortal guardian spirit that lived inside fireplaces or furnaces in people's homes. It has been believed that it guards the fires and in doing so has a link to the ancestors. Popielnik looked like a hunch-backed dwarf with a cat's head and grey striped fur, and were very grumpy and easily angered. If treated unkindly by humans or if annoyed by the sounds of an oncoming storm, it was known to cause serious fires that would burn places to the ground, which the Popielnik would then spitefully haunt, keeping people from wanting to rebuild. It was therefore very impoartant to treat all fireplaces in your house with uttermost care and respect. Apparently there were some holidays when people would take the Popielnik out of their homes and carry it on display to celebrate ancestral fires. Popielnik's name comes from the Polish word for "ash" (popiół), and is the same word for the ash-accumulating container under the grate of a hearth or fireplace.

Chochlik

Origin: Slavic

A house spirit that looks very much like an ordinary housecat, but can also become invisible. A Chochlik usually has a longer tail and limbs than a regular cat, highly expressive eyes with prominent double eyelids, greater strength, and unexpected outbursts of energy. They are mischievous and like to play tricks on people, and will also eat some of your food and supplies. If you treat a Chochlik well and keep it fed, then it will defend your house from other potentially harmful spirits. But if you mistreat a Chochlik, then it will go on a rampage around your house, knocking things off shelves, breaking dishes, and even overturning furniture. Given that they look so much like common domesticated cats, it is best to treat all cats well, lest you accidentally anger a Chochlik.

BASTET
Origin: Egyptian

Bastet (sometimes Bast) was an ancient Egyptian cat goddess of fertility, protection against evil spirits and disease, protector of lower (Northern) Egypt, and protector of Ra and consequently the Pharaoh. Originally associated with Sekhmet, later tradition placed more distinction between them, so Bastet is represented by the domesticated cat while Sekhmet takes the form of a lioness. Bastet is portrayed in combat with the snake god Apophis (or Apep), likely related to domestic cats in ancient Egypt being valued for, among other things, their ability to fight off snakes. Bastet's qualities of protection against evil spirits and diseases also probably comes from the domestic cat's fending off of rodents and other vermin. A powerful symbol of cats from a culture that valued them highly.

Other Names:
Bastet, Bast, B'sst, Baast, Ubaste, Baset

Wag-by-the-Way

Origin: Celtic

Wag-by-the-way is a small cat-like faery or sprite from Scottish folklore that has a long tail that they wag when angry or upset, and they may also throw objects at people who irritate them. Despite this, they are considered helpful and beneficial, even going so far as to perform household chores. They guard entryways, and even roads in the Scottish lowlands. Like ordinary cats, they seek warmth and are usually to be found by fireplaces, as it is said that they have a cold-blooded nature, and are consequently often covered in ash. They are considered very loyal to the families they choose to protect, and will do so for many generations, but usually only within the same household, and do not follow younger family members who move away from their ancestral homes.

Cath Palug
Origin: Celtic

A legendarily horrible cat from Gwynedd in Welsh folklore which haunts the Isle of Anglesey. It had already allegedly killed 180 soldiers when a man named Sir Kay was sent to the island to dispatch it. The name likely means "scratching cat" but may also have other shades of meaning. Cath Palug is said to favor water, and is sometimes interpreted as a combination of cat and fish. It appears in the legendarium of current and former Celtic lands, including old French. In various tales, a Cath Palug or its analogue either kills or is killed by King Arthur. It is also said to have been born of a white sow called "Henwen" (old white) in Welsh tradition.

Other Names:
Cath Paluc, Cath Baluq, Cath Balwq, Paluq's Cat

Yule Cat

Origin: Icelandic

The Yule Cat, or Jólakötturinn, is an Icelandic Christmas legend that has appeared in Icelandic folklore for an indeterminate amount of time, likely since near the beginning of the Christianization of Iceland. Popularized by a poem by Icelandic poet Jóhannes úr Kötlum, the tale of the Yule Cat has taken deep root in Icelandic culture that continues to this day. It is said that the Yule Cat, a gigantic cat larger than a house, will catch people instead of mice around Christmas time, seeking out those who have not received clothing as a gift. Clothing was a traditional gift for those who had worked hard during the year, be they children or labourers. This is likely related to the historical importance of the local textile industry and the general value of warm clothing in a cold climate. Thus the Yule Cat would effectively seek out the lazy from around the entire country. So be grateful for those socks you get for Christmas, they might actually be saving your life!

Other Names:
Jólakötturinn

WARGIN
Origin: Slavic

Wargin was an enormous black cat demon in Slavic mythology. Apparently he was the actual king of all cats. He had deeply black fur and burning embers in his eyes. He moved without making any noise and was able to enter any room or place, no matter how secure. He liked to be among humans, being beloved and pampered, constantly changing owners. He would find humans and offer his company and blessings, bringing luck and fortune to them; however this came at a terrible price. After a few months or weeks of having this cat around, anyone dealing with Wargin would have their minds poisoned by greed and paranoia, which in turn made them push their family and friends away; and eventually all their fortune would be gone too. Alone and desperate, Wargin's victim would then die in pure torture – Wargin's final spell being having insects (such as wasps, butterflies, moths, or others) be birthed in it's victim's head, summoned by Wargin's purrs. This poor human would die a terrible and painful death. Wargin and the effects of his activities could only be dealt with by a shaman or a healer who knew secret spells that could not only drive him out of the yard but also destroy him.

KASHA

Origin: Japanese

Kasha (literally "flame cart" or "fire chariot"), is a Japanese yokai that is said to carry away the remains of the dead. They are depicted as tiger-headed with a flaming tail, but normally take the form of an ordinary housecat, where they share some overlap of mythology with the Banekeno and Nekomata, perhaps because it is nearly impossible to distinguish them until they make their move. They are at least as large as a human, bipedal, and appear during funeral services to steal the bodies of the dead before they can be cremated. This superstition has led to decoy cremation services being held where stones are used in place of the corpse in the hopes that the Kasha will mistakenly carry away the stones, so that the actual remains can later be cremated in peace. Kasha may also be interpreted as vengeful spirits that carry away the souls of the sinful for torment in the afterlife.

Cactus Cat
Origin: North American

The Cactus Cat is another "fearsome critter" (see the entry on Ball-Tailed Cat) from the Southwest of North America. They resemble the great cats in size and shape, and are covered head to tail in long spines similar to that of a cactus. Their tails also branch off in cactus-like fashion, are covered in spikes, and can be swung as a weapon. They have long claws on their front limbs, which they use to slash open cacti in their area; they perform this action in a circuit, returning to the first cacti by the time the cactus juice has fermented in to an alcoholic drink, which they consume for its intoxicating effects, and spend the night howling drunkenly. Humans attempting to harvest this alcohol must be cautious to do so before the Cactus Cat returns, and many have reportedly met their deaths at the claws or tail of such a cat.

Other Names:
Felis spinobiblulosus

MANEKI-NEKO
Origin: Japanese

Maneki Neko meaning "beckoning cat" or "inviting cat" is a Japanese cultural symbol of good fortune and prosperity. It is sometimes mistaken as being Chinese in origin owing to its popularity in Chinese and other Asian markets in Western countries. It is often depicted with a koban, an early Japanese gold coin. Representations of the Maneki-Neko are typically, though not exclusively, three-dimensional (e.g. statues, wooden or plastic figures), and are most commonly placed next to entrances or in windows facing the street from which customers would enter. They are also placed inside the home to bring good luck and fortune to the household, with these figures holding up the right paw instead of the left (usually they are depicted holding up the left paw for business, and the right paw for home). There are a few origin tales for the Maneki Neko. The most popular story is that a shop owner took in a stray cat, which liked to spend time in the shop window, raising its paw at passing people, who would notice the cat and enter the shop as a result, thus bringing prosperity to the shop owner. It is noteworthy that in Japanese culture the hand gesture to beckon someone forth "temaneki" is different than in Western cultures, which may cause the latter to interpret it as more of a "waving goodbye" motion.

Underwater Panther

Origin: Native North American

The Underwater Panther or Mishibijiw (various spellings) is a mythological cat creature found in the traditions of several Native American tribes, especially those from around the Great Lakes. They are seen as a counterpart of and in opposition to the Thunderbirds, where the Thunderbirds have the dominion of the sky, the Underwater Panthers have the dominion of the underworld, including under the water's surface, and are considered the most powerful of the underworld beings. They are described as having large feline bodies, with horns or antlers on its otherwise cat-like head, scales or sometimes feathers on their backs, and very long serpent-like tails. They sometimes share other traits with serpents, such as producing a serpent-like hissing noise rather than feline sounds. They are protectors of the copper deposits around the great lakes area, and removing copper from the region is an affront to the Underwater Panthers. Several local tribes hold Michipicoten Island in Lake Superior to be home to the Underwater Panthers.

Other Names:

Mishibizhiw, Mishipizhiw, Mishipizheu, Mishupishu, Mishepishu, Michipeshu, Mishibijiw

BAJUN
Origin: Slavic

The Bajun cat or Bayun cat is a very large cat from Russian folklore. Its name comes from the word "lull" and also "tell", and as such the Bajun cat is said to lull people to sleep with its voice, both by singing songs and telling stories, and its voice also has healing properties. It's name may also bear a connection to Bayan, which is both the name of an instrument and of a mythical Russian storyteller to whom many ancient tales are attributed. The Bajun cat is said to sit atop an iron pillar in a barren forest where no other animals live. In various tales it is said to be confronted by "Ivan Tsarevich" or "Andrei the shooter", who is sent to capture it. Capturing a Bajun cat is a sort of fool's errand in Russian culture, said to be an impossible task given to someone in order to destroy them. To capture the Bajun cat, one must wear iron gloves and an iron cap, or multiple iron caps; which have the effect of either outright protecting one from the cat, or by tiring it out by forcing it to break so much iron, at which point it becomes exhausted and can be captured. In some tales, the hero returns to the King (or Tsar) with the cat, and uses the healing properties of it's voice to cure the King or some other important person. The Bajun cat also appears in tales where a mother has children who have trouble sleeping, so she leaves out some wine and the last bits of a pie to lure the Bajun cat so it will come to the house and cause the children to fall asleep. In other stories, Bajun cat is the personal cat of Baba Yaga. The tales of the Bajun cat appear to be especially ancient, possibly several thousands of years, repeatedly featuring iron during a time when the region was presumed by modern archaeologists to not yet be in the iron age.

OTHER NAMES:
Bayun, Kot Bajarz

Demon Cat
Origin: North American (D.C.)

The Demon Cat (or D.C.) is a ghost cat claimed to haunt the Capitol Building and White House in Washington D.C. (get it?) In the early years of the history of these buildings, cats would regularly be employed to keep the halls free from rodents and other pests, and the Demon Cat is one such cat who never left, even in death. There are in fact cat's paw prints to be found in concrete in some areas of these buildings. Sightings of the Demon Cat in these buildings are peppered through their history; security guards or others on watch would report seeing an ordinary-looking cat which would then swell up to the size of an elephant. These reports were usually attributed to drunken guards who obtained their positions through nepotism. The last official report of a Demon Cat sighting was from the World War II era. Despite this, the stories persist to this day.

Other Names:
D.C., Demon Cat of Washington D.C.

MAJKI
Origin: Slavic

Majki were small beings that inhabited Slavic forests and caves, seldom interacted with humans, and were never seen. The evidence of their presence was strange circular tracks left in forest meadows, which apparently were from their dancing at night. If they ever got close to a human dwelling, they did so only to play tricks on humans. Their favorite thing was to sing cat arias in the middle of the night, especially whenever humans were about to engage in amorous activities, which were usually spoiled by the terrible and loud cat noises from the Majki. Apparently they often did this to husbands that were about to be unfaithful, foiling their plans of infidelity.

OTHER NAMES:
Mawki, Newki

SPLINTERCAT
Origin: North American

The Splintercat is formidable feline "fearsome critter" (see the entry on Ball-Tailed Cat) from North America, whose range is said to extend across much of the mainland United States. There are no reports of it having been seen by humans, but anyone who has been to an old forest has likely witnessed evidence of its activities. It spends its time leaping or flying between trees, and will deliberately crash in to a tree with its thickened skull in order to break it open and find food, such as small animals living in the tree or honey from a beehive. This leaves tree trunks split off and stumps uprooted, damage mundanely attributed to strong winds and storms. There is in fact a "Splintercat Creek" in Oregon, South-West of Mount Hood, which was apparently named after the "fearsome critter" by one T.H. Sherrard, who was supervisor of the Mount Hood National Forest around the late 19th and early 20th centuries, and did so in order to honor the tale of the Splintercat, of which he was a fan.

Other Names:
Nasusossificatus arbordemolieus

Pauca Billee

Origin: Indian / World

From Hindi "pankha billi" meaning "winged cat", the Pauca Billee is an alleged cryptid and historical curiosity that appears in various places around the world over approximately the last two centuries. Popularized somewhat in India in 1868 after a man named Alexander Gibson allegedly shot one and exhibited its dried skin at a Bombay Asiatic Society meeting. Skeptics said the skin had belonged to either a flying fox (a type of bat) or a colugo (a flying lemur), though Gibson claimed it was an entirely new species. There are numerous newspaper articles from the 1800's and 1900's with stories and photographs of living domesticated cats, or taxidermized specimens, claiming to be cats with wings. It is most likely that these living cats merely had either birth defects and/or badly matted fur, and that the taxidermized specimens were either of the same like or outright frauds. Still, the idea of a flying or winged cat has appeared in various mythologies. Two unnamed flying (though not explicitly winged) cats pulled Freyja's chariot in Norse mythology. The Goddess Bastet of Egyptian mythology was often depicted with wings. And both the Sphinx and Lamassu in Egyptian and Assyrian mythologies, respectively, were feline-bodied and winged, though with human heads and not strictly "cats" per se. Cats with wings have appeared in innumerable works of art and fiction, and there is something about a cat with wings that stimulates the imagination.

Other Names:
Winged Cat

WAMPUS
Origin: Native North American

Wampus is the name given to a mythological cat or a cat-woman in Cherokee and Appalachian folklore. Variations of the Wampus story exist across several regions, and separating details can be difficult. Two main stories seem to tell the origin of the Wampus. In the first story, a demon is terrorizing a village, slaying many of their best warriors, including the husband of a certain woman who then vows revenge on the demon. She is given several magical tools by the elders, including a bobcat mask which will grant her the appearance of a ferocious cat in order to help defeat the demon, which she does, after which her spirit remains in the area in order to protect her kin from future dangers, usually taking the feline form to do so. Another tale claims that Wampus was a Cherokee woman who snuck in to a secret ritual she, as a woman, was forbidden from witnessing, and then in punishment was cursed by the shamans to become a terrible cat monster, banished from her village, doomed to roam the wild and sometimes attacking men in her grief and anger. In this version, reading from the Bible aloud apparently keeps the Wampus away.

Other Names:
Gallywampus, Whistling Wampus

Bog Cat
Origin: Celtic

It is a common belief that black cats are bad luck, but in some Celtic areas, particularly Ireland, they are considered to be the height of good luck. The Bog Cat is an Irish mythical cat said to roam Lough Neagh, the largest lake in all the British Isles, West of Belfast in Northern Ireland. The Bog Cat is larger than an ordinary domesticated cat, usually with a pot belly, little to no chin, fur that runs back-to-front, long rear limbs for navigating the bog, and a tail kinked in one or more places. Their solitary nature and cunning elusiveness has led to the belief that good fortune will follow anyone who even witnesses one. They are more recently associated with Saint Brendan, and are said to be born on Saint Patrick's Day; but the origin of the Irish Bog Cat long predates the introduction of Christianity to the region. To this day, lucky black cat figures can be purchased as souvenirs and trinkets in Ireland.

SELECTED BIBLIOGRAPHY:

Below is a recommended further reading and list of reference books the author found instrumental in doing reseach for this book. This is not the only reference used for each subject, but the most useful ones you may enjoy in doing further reading.

Slavic Creatures*:
Linkner, Tadeusz. 1998. "Słowiańskie Bogi i Demony"
Podgórscy, Barbara & Adam. 2018. "Wielka Księga Demonów Polskich"
Vargas, Witold & Zych, Pawel. 2018. "Bestiariusz Słowiański: Część Pierwsza i Druga"
*books listed above are in polish

Fearsome Critters of North America**:
Tryon, Henry H. 1939. "Fearsome Critters"
Cox, William T. 1910. "Fearsome Creatures of the Lumberwoods"
**courtesy of Lumberwoods Unnatural History Museum
http://www.lib.lumberwoods.com

Winged Cat:
Hartwell, Sarah. 2001-2017. "Winged Cats - Historical Reports"
http://messybeast.com/winged-cats-1.htm

Japanese Yokai:
Meyer, Matthew. "The Online Database of Japanese Ghosts and Monsters". https://yokai.com

Disclaimer:
This book is a work of art. It is not intended as a scientific manual or research source. Care was taken to ensure information is as complete and accurate as possible, but is in no way exhaustive or definitive.

Alex Kujawa is a graphic artist and illustrator based in the Chicago area, where she lives with her husband and cats. She was born in Poland and moved to the United States in her teens, where she attended Harper College and Judson University. Her personal style has evolved as a blending of creepy and beautiful, being inspired by the art nouveau movement, as well as horror and dark fantasy. She usually works in ink with pen and marker on paper, and adds digital color. She began her series of illustrated folklore books in 2017, but has been been drawing and researching strange creatures and stories for far longer. To see more of Alex's art, follow her on social media through AlexKujawa.com

WHEEJAWA PUBLISHING
Second Edition

Copyright ©2024 by Alex Kujawa
Illustrated by Alex Kujawa
Written by Alex Kujawa and Scott Wheeler

www.AlexKujawa.com

OTHER BOOKS IN THIS SERIES:

♥ **31 FEMALE GHOSTS, MONSTERS, & DEMONS FROM AROUND THE WORLD:**
Dives into the theme of female folktales and mythical creatures from around the world - ghosts, demons, monsters, and the like. This book contains 31 illustrations and background information on each particular creature.
ISBN 979-8-9866079-1-7

☠ **31 GHOST STORIES:**
Ranging from famous to more obscure and even including a personal story, this book contains 31 illustrations and background information on each particular ghost. All ghost stories are tied to places and a majority of the ghosts are named, and circumstances of their deaths explained.
ISBN 979-8-9866079-2-4

🪶 **31 SLAVIC BEINGS OF MYTH & MAGIC:**
Probably the most intensively researched book, choosing the theme of Slavic Beings of Myth and Magic as a means for the author to learn more about her Slavic pagan heritage. This book contains 31 illustrations and background information on the particular being - including deities, spirits, and creatures.
ISBN 979-8-9866079-3-1

www.ingramcontent.com/pod-product-compliance
Lightning Source LLC
LaVergne TN
LVHW061631070526
838199LV00071B/6643